# PIG CITY

AFTER THE DUST SETTLED

# PIG CITY

JONATHAN MARY-TODD

darbycreek

MINNEAPOLIS

Darby Creek
A division of Lerner Publishing Group, Inc.
241 First Avenue North
Minneapolis, MN 55401 U.S.A.

Website address: www.lernerbooks.com

Cover and interior images: © iStockphoto.com/patrimonio
designs limited (wild boar); © iStockphoto.com/Lou Oates
(antique blank album page, background); © iStockphoto.com/
Anagramm, (burnt edge, background); © iStockphoto.com/
Evgeny Kuklev (aged notebook background); © iStockphoto.
com/kizilkayaphotos (coffee stain); © iStockphoto.com/José Luis
Gutiérrez (Fingerprints); © iStockphoto.com/Bojan Stamenkovic
(burnt paper background).

Main body text set in Janson Text LT Std 55 Roman 12/17.5.
Typeface provided by Adobe Systems.

Mary-Todd, Jonathan.
　　Pig City / by Jonathan Mary-Todd.
　　　　p.　cm. — (After the dust settled)
　　Summary: When snow drives Malik, Beckley, Emma,
and Wendell into Des Moines, Iowa, they are taken in by a
Coalition that is caught between an anti-electricity, cult-like
group and brutes who raise pigs to trade, feeding them on
children.
　　ISBN: 978–0–7613–8328–4 (lib. bdg. : alk. paper)
　　[1. Survival—Fiction. 2. Interpersonal relations—Fiction.
3. Civilization—Fiction. 4. Des Moines (Iowa)—Fiction.
5. Science fiction.] I. Title.
PZ7.M36872Pig 2012
[Fic]—dc23　　　　　　　　　　　　　2012001405

Manufactured in the United States of America
1 – BP – 7/15/12

To G.B.C., Ice Age Club,
and other Iowan coalitions
to which I have belonged

## CHAPTER ONE

I'd been lying under a blanket on top of overgrown grass when the first snowflakes touched my face. I sat up and shivered. All around me, flakes were coming down. Melting as soon as they landed. But enough were falling that the patch of sand a body's-length away from me was dotted with white.

I turned to look behind me. "Beckley. Wake up."

Beckley swept the stringy brown hair from her face, rubbed her eyes, and put on her pair of cracked glasses.

"Oh dear," she said. "Well, we'd better move fast today. It'll only get tougher once the snow starts to stick."

Her sister, Emma, sat up next to her, wrapped in a patched-together sleeping bag. She trembled in the cold like a rabbit.

"We should've broken the lock on that toolshed last night," Beckley murmured. "It would've been worth it. Look at Emma, she's freezing."

"We?" Wendell's voice crept over from the other side of Emma. "Malik and me always do that stuff, us boys!"

"And *I've* caught our last dozen meals. That's just you earning your keep, Wendy," Beckley replied.

"Don't call me that."

Wendell had walked with us for the last season or so. We spent a few moons moving east together. Lately we'd been in what Beckley said was probably the place people called Iowa. The land was flat, and it would go along without ending. Strong winds hit us most days while we walked over fallen stalks of wild corn. Most of them were half mush, no good for eating. Our hungry stretches had gotten longer, broken up sometimes by squirrel roasts.

"Okay, now this next part's important. Emma, are you listening? 'At the moment you see a spark drift downward, touch the tinder'—that's the husks, in our case—'and blow softly onto the bundle.'"

Beckley and her sister stood above a pile of dried corn husks we'd collected, trying to block out the wind. Emma struck the dull side of a blade from my pocketknife against a chunk of flint.

"'You should begin to see a wisp of smoke rise from the ti—' um, husks, 'as well as a glow that will grow larger as the fire spreads.' Uhh . . . keep trying with the flint in the meantime."

Beckley read aloud from *Gene Matterhorn's Wilderness Survival Guidebook*. She was the best reader in the group—the one who really liked to. We'd taken the guide, along with my pocketknife, some of the blankets, and most of our clothes from a place to the west of us. The Frontier Motel. The Frontier was where Beckley and I had spent most of our younger years. Emma was even born there.

My mother had stopped at the Frontier the same time Beckley and Emma's parents did. People were worried, my mother said. Phones had stopped working. The Frontier was a place where people could stop and rest before they got where they were going. When everybody started to panic, people like our parents got off the road there.

They met with rumors of fighting in the east, disasters. Some people headed back out right away, searching for news. My mother stayed. Since I left the place, I've never met anyone who knew for sure what happened.

The Frontier was a safe place. Nothing else was around it but stretches of trees and a gravel road. After the world our parents were used to stopped working, they and some others started to build a life together.

Soon enough, my mom said, any fuel nearby was gone anyway. There was no driving somewhere else. Beckley's dad told everybody after some trips beyond the motel's woods that we should all keep to the Frontier. It wasn't 'til the last of our parents passed that we set out. We weren't looking for anything. It was just that we didn't feel like we could stay.

· · ·

Wendell talked with a mouth full of squirrel meat.

"What'd you say this place is?"

"It's called a golf course," Beckley said, tilting the remains of the squirrel above the morning fire.

"What's *that*?"

"It's—a place where people played a game. Called golf."

"What's that? How do you know that?"

"At the place where we got the Matterhorn book, there were some other books," Beckley said. "One was called *How to Improve Your Golf Swing*. Or, I think the name was longer, but that was part of it."

"What?"

Beckley and Wendell both frowned. They made each other confused a few times a day.

"There are supposed to be holes around, but I think the grass is covering them up," Beckley added.

"Hm," Wendell said. For some reason, that seemed to satisfy him.

*Wendell might've never played a game in his life*, I thought afterward. Wiry, red-haired, he had a hook-shaped scar around one eye. It was a mark from a snakebite, from his life before we met him.

We'd run into Wendell while we were looking for Emma a few moons back. She'd been taken by an old man and a pack of wild kids—a pack Wendell belonged to. The group scavenged, stole, and killed. There were probably a lot more people in the world like them.

After we got Emma back, Wendell came with us. He seemed like he'd seen too much wrong to keep running with his old pack. But he still sometimes moved more like a wild animal. He'd lived in the woods longer than the rest of us—had grown up there.

Together we all kept moving. On better days, we even felt hopeful, even if we didn't know what we were moving toward. Staying safe took work. But after years at the Frontier, we got to see something new most days. I liked that part.

The snow fell harder as morning ended. The sky was gray, like the ceiling of an endless cave. Around the time I couldn't feel the squirrel meat in my belly anymore, we saw a wide sign. Metal-green with cracked white letters. *DES MOINES: POPULATION 200,538.*

"Hmph," Beckley said, flicking her compass back and forth between two fingers. "I wish we still had our map. That number's bigger than most cities we've come across. This place probably goes on for miles. Still . . . maybe if we move south for a bit, we can totally avoid the more populated places. Potentially populated, that is."

We stayed out of cities. Anytime we could, we went around them. In cities there were blocks, and on blocks there were buildings. In buildings there were floors, and on floors there were rooms. People carved up the places and fought to keep whatever they said was theirs. Cities meant fighting.

But as I watched a cloud of breath pass in front of my face, I felt, in my gut, a move forward coming.

"Beckley," I said. "We've been walking on open ground, day after day. If the snow keeps falling, it's only gonna get harder to find places to make camp. I don't know how we're gonna stay warm out here."

She squinted through her cracked lenses. "What are you saying?" Then she waved a hand and kept going. "Malik, we're surrounded by farmland—"

"We were on a golf course," Wendell added.

"We're *surrounded* by farmland. We can walk until we find a farm*house*, and . . ."

She pulled out *Gene Matterhorn's Wilderness Survival Guidebook* and rapped on it with her knuckles. "*Matterhorn* has ways we can deal with this. We can build up wood and make a lean-to, a snow trench if it gets deep, or—"

Emma's teeth started to chatter. She clamped up when her sister looked her way. Beckley's shoulders dropped.

"All right," she sighed. "Hello, Des Moines."

# CHAPTER TWO

"Locust Avenue," Beckley said. "*Now* I can relax."

"Huh?" I asked.

"Locusts. Insects, mean ones."

"Mean how?"

"They chew up everything in their path. So I've read," Beckley said. "It's a bad omen. That's all I mean."

"You said it was an insect," Wendell said.

Beckley sighed and stomped a few steps ahead without saying anything else.

A thumb's-depth of snow had fallen since we'd moved into the city. It was starting to stick. The buildings began to get taller as we walked. At first they'd mostly been small, box-shaped, one floor high. Sometimes a row of boxy buildings with large windows and broken, burned-out signs at the top. But in the distance, after a long, soft slope, we could see places much taller, looking over what had to be the center of the city. I tried to take in as much as I could.

Beckley paused in front of us and waited for us to catch up.

"The compass says we're still headed east. Which is good. But since I've lost sight of our short-term trajectory, where do you guys say we stop?"

For a moment, I felt the foolish kind of reckless that comes with hiding out for too long. The wanting something different, to just *go*, see places besides cornfields. I pushed the feeling out of my head. The problem was, I couldn't think of something else. Nowhere else *to* go but further into the city. I pointed toward the cluster of tall buildings ahead. Maybe taller than any we'd ever seen before.

"There," I said.

Beckley grabbed hold of Emma's hand. "I hope one of you has a plan for when we get down there, because I don't." With her other hand, Beckley began to swing a weapon she'd made, her bola, low above the ground. Her second one—she'd lost the first to the pack Wendell used to run with. She'd put the new bola together from pond rocks and old bootlaces. Watching the rocks dangle at the end of the threads, I felt around in my pocket for the smooth casing of my knife. The city was still, but I couldn't say she was wrong to worry.

Like Beckley, Wendell seemed nervous as the tall buildings got closer. But rather than her stiff, straight steps, he made a sideways swoop as he went forward, small shifts to the left or the right. His head wouldn't stay fixed in one direction for more than a breath or two. Wendell and Beckley had bonded over what Beckley called navigation—finding a course and following it. Even if they annoyed

each other now, she'd helped put him at ease a
season ago. The fixed trail of a city street put
them both on guard.

"Where are the people?" Emma asked
after a length of silence. The sunlight had
started to get dimmer behind snow clouds. My
legs ached from walking.

"It's snowing out," Beckley said.
"Everybody's inside, warming up!"

Her little sister frowned. "Don't talk to me
like that. That's not how you talk to Malik!
This place is weird."

"She's got sort of a point," I said. "It *is*
weird we haven't seen *anybody*, right? Maybe
it's totally deserted. Could be a good way to
spend winter, making camp here. If we can
find some food."

"When can we stop?" asked Emma.

"Soon," said Beckley. "When we find a
good place. Let's keep an eye out, yeah?"

"Yeah," said Wendell.

"Fine with me," I added. Snot ran from my
nose in a wet crawl. I rubbed each of my arms
with the opposite hand to keep them warm.

It was maybe the cold, thin air that kept us from smelling the stink for so long. It came on like just the *thought* of a bad smell—a hint to get alert and start sniffing.

Wendell coughed hard and spun his head left and right. Beckley pulled a scarf she'd made from motel bedsheets tight over her nose and mouth.

"Whht sss thhht?" she mumbled.

"Stink," Wendell said. "Like animals."

It got worse, muscling its way across the open air. I took heavy breaths between my cracked lips and tried not to let more of the smell in my nose. At the left edge of my sight I saw movement, sudden, short. I turned toward a tall, empty structure that looked like a place for cars. Each level hung forward like a pair of eyebrows, throwing a shadow on the one below it.

A few lengths ahead, Emma skipped around, taking short jumps. She pinched her nose with one hand and made circles in the air with the other. I stopped and looked down. Each footprint along Emma's path was like the splash of a rock dropped in water. The outline of a larger foot, the bottom of a grown man's boot, surrounded the marks from the tiny treads of her shoes like a ripple. The curves of the larger footprint were crisp, unsoftened by the falling snow. Recent.

"Emma!" I called out. "Stop! Beckley, your sister found footprints."

Beckley rubbed specks of snow off her glasses, and her eyes widened. "Emma! Why didn't you say something?"

"I was *skipping*," Emma said.

Beckley reddened. "*This* is why I don't talk—"

A rush of air swept down Locust Street, lifting up the top layer of new snow from the ground and stinging our faces. I shut my eyes, and when I reopened them, two men stood in front of us. Pink-skinned, tall and wide, round hairless heads. Faces like reflections of each other's. The men wore tan overalls, thick tan jackets. One held a rust-colored chain, the other a crowbar. He pointed with the crowbar to Beckley's bola.

"Gimme that. The weapon. Any of the rest you've got."

"Not kidding," the other man said.

"Then get together, all of you," continued the first man. "Form a line. You're coming with us."

# CHAPTER THREE

*B*eckley grabbed hold of Emma's arm and pulled her sister behind her. Then, under the eyes of the two bald men, she held the bola out in front of her. One of them giggled. I kept my fingers pressed on the knife in my pocket.

"Is that everything?" the other man said, while his brother pushed Wendell against Emma. Wendell's shaky hand made a fist, and the large man frowned, grunted, and took Wendell by the wrist. He shoved him against the rest of us again.

"Last chance."

My eyes met Beckley's, and she shook her head no with a slight jerk. I let the knife slide to the bottom of my pocket.

We started to walk, one man on each side of our group. We took a turn past the entrance of the parking garage.

"Where are you taking us?" Beckley asked. Maybe she was stalling, waiting for me to act. But I was curious, too. The stink got even worse.

The two men ignored Beckley and talked across us to each other.

"Hey, Daryll. What did Mr. Tyson say about the traders?"

"Didn't talk to Mr. Tyson. Talked to Hank Bradley."

"Oh."

"Yeah."

"What did Hank Bradley say about the traders?"

"He says they should be stopping in the next week. Bringing new tools, maybe some heaters. Going by Hank's calendar."

"Oh."

"Yeah."

"Hank say how much pig he thinks they'll want?"

"No. Prob'ly a lot."

"Heh. Yeah. Bum timing."

"Huh?"

"All the snow."

"Oh. Yeah. Maybe it'll just get worse though."

"Yeah. Glad we don't have to come to *them*."

"Heh. Yeah."

"Think Mr. Tyson will ever let the boys from Saint Louis trade with him again?"

"Nuh-uh. No way. Not after one of 'em tried to sneak a knife past Hank Bradley during the pat-down. Mr. Tyson says rules are rules. Can't forget that it's a business."

"Huh. Dang. I miss that jug wine those boys used to bring up."

"Heh. Me too."

We walked between the men for a few steps before the one on the left stopped.

"Duane," he whispered. "You do the pat-down?"

"What?" said Duane.

"The pat-down. On these kids."

"We can hear you," said Beckley.

"Shut up," said Daryll. "Duane—check 'em again before we get back. Or Hank'll get mad."

"Okay."

Duane giggled again, and I fingered my hidden pocketknife. He lifted Emma off the ground with one arm and tapped the outsides of her pockets with the other. I pictured the blade poking through the bald man's hand when he went to check me. Then Duane set Emma down—on the left side of him, keeping hold of her coat's collar while he moved to pat down Wendell. *If we run*, I thought, *Emma'd have a wall between her and the rest of us.*

On one side of the street ahead, another big, open structure, like the other I'd seen, ended at the edge of an alleyway. An unbroken stretch of buildings lay along the other side. Daryll, on my right side, checked the first of my coat pockets while we all stepped slowly onward. Then, a flicker of light from the alleyway.

"Cheee-arge!" a big voice boomed. Emma shrieked and ducked as a burst of flame rushed left to right across our path. Duane's tan jacket caught fire, and he whipped it off, kneeling down to pat snow on his smoky undershirt.

I jumped back, pulling Wendell with me. The fire came from a large lighter, someone in a helmet spraying a mist of something into the flame and sending it roaring outward. He slid out of the alley, standing in a wheeled metal cart. Deep chuckles grew louder behind him as a man even bigger than the brothers pushed the cart along.

"Oof!"

The cart's wheels skipped across something buried in the snow, and the person in the helmet toppled out, his spray can chucked into the snow. By then the man behind the cart was charging us, waving a narrow length of wood above his head.

"Retreat! Retreat! Heh heh!"

"It's the Captain!" Daryll shouted to Duane, who slipped in the snow after diving for Emma.

The man who had pushed the cart wore a bright orange beard, a stocking cap, and a thick blue overcoat. He smacked down the end of Daryll's chain. Beckley and I turned to stare at each other, mouths open.

"Forget it," Daryll mumbled, dodging a thwack from the bearded man. Duane tumbled through the snow, yanking his brother's collar, and the two of them took off down the alley the cart had come through. The boy who'd fallen out of the cart rushed to his feet, collecting the spray can and flicking at the lighter. He looked the same age as me and Beckley, with a thin, pointed chin. Strands of brown hair dangled under his helmet.

"'S alright, Lucas, we drove 'em off," the bearded man said. "Go on an' run!" he shouted into the alley. "Pig slop."

He turned back to the younger one. "You hear me shout at the start? I thought of that on the spot. Heckuva sense of the dramatic, if I say so myself."

"Very dramatic," the boy in the helmet said. "I'm not doing the cart thing again."

The bearded man turned to me, Beckley, and Emma. He looked at us, curious, then put his fists at his hips with a grin.

"Pleasure to make your acquaintance," he said. "Carl Fitzsimmons. Most people call me the Captain."

# CHAPTER FOUR

The Captain took us right, shuffling away from where the bald men had run and down a side street.

"Locust Avenue's usually all right," he said, "'specially in the daytime. Those twins musta been feelin' extra frisky. I wouldn't head past Grand if I was you, though. It's a few blocks of no-man's-land from there. And then of course, Pig City." He paused. "You're not from around here, I'm assuming."

"No," Beckley said. "Not exactly." She had

plucked her bola back out of one of the bald men's pockets in the confusion earlier and had been twirling it ever since. She pocketed it and turned to the boy our age. He had taken off his helmet and put on a pair of rectangular glasses. Gray tape held them together in the middle. "You could've given us some severe burns with that torch."

"I—I didn't know who I was aiming—" he stammered. He nodded to the Captain. "His idea." Then he looked down to Emma. She walked between her sister and the boy. The snakebite scar showed along the side of her mouth, a mark from the old man who had led Wendell's pack. If the boy saw it, he didn't make a face. Maybe he'd seen worse.

"I'm sorry," he said, soft. Beckley lowered her shoulders a bit.

"Don't be bashful, Lucas," the Captain chuckled. "Lucas here had the germ of the idea. Idea Man is what I call him. Besides,"— he laughed again—"all's well that ends well, and I believe we saved yer butts!"

We turned again onto a street that ran alongside Locust Avenue. Most of the buildings were covered with windows and took up long stretches of the block. I gazed at a giant mess of metal bars, blue, looking like a different thing every few steps—a fishhook, or the umbrellas we'd sometimes find in dumps. Snow was stacked a few inches high along the bars, and it dropped off in clumps.

"Public art," the Captain said. "I'll leave it to Idea Man to explain that one."

To the right of the big blue umbrella I saw dim lights in the windows of a couple buildings—candle flames. The Captain nodded to a man standing outside the building nearest us. The man held a long metal pipe, and his face was wrapped up in two scarves.

"Evenin', Mitch," said the Captain.

"Captain," said the man.

"You wouldn't believe what we seen out there tonight."

"I bet."

"Mitch is one of our finest lookouts," the Captain said to us. "Hey, Mitch," he called out again. "Know where I can find the Mayor?"

"Condos," the man said. "Usual place."

The Captain waved us toward the next building over. The place shot high up, with overhangs lining it like a ribcage.

"Most of us live in one of the rooms along the block here. Easiest to share food, news that way." He pointed forward, up the street to his left. "We use the Civic Center mostly for group meetings and the like, least in wintertime, but it's got some suitable living spaces for the more transient types."

We stepped through the double doors of the second building on the block, wind rushing in behind us. The doors' big sheets of glass were cracked most of the way through, boarded up on the side that faced the street. The Captain began hustling up the nearest stairway, dripping muddy snow on the tile.

Beckley glanced from side to side. "Um— excuse me," she said. "What . . . is this place? I mean—who are we meeting? I—" She looked to Lucas, and he opened his mouth like he was midway to an answer. The Captain chuckled again.

"Guess I'm getting ahead of myself. We've

taken to calling it the Patchwork Coalition of Des Moines, Iowa. Although a coalition's a thing. And this place is more of a place. Er— it's sort of a thing and a place."

Beckley and I looked at each other with puzzled brows. Wendell nodded a few times at the man.

"It's a safe space," the Captain continued. "People gotta live somewhere. Some of us've been living 'round here since before . . ." He frowned. "Well, since before the end of polite society. Ask me, we shouldn't discount the idea of extra-*terr*-estrial intervention. Anyway, we look after each other—nearly anyone who wants to stay. Hrm—but here's the Mayor."

He stopped in front of a door near the end of a hall two floors up.

"I'm not sure that answered any of my questions," Beckley whispered to me.

The woman who answered the bearded man's knocks was pale and lean. Lines ran down her face. Her black hair was cut short. She looked around the age my mother had been when she passed.

"Presentin' Coalition Mayor Catherine Forsythe," the Captain said. The woman rolled her eyes.

"Catherine is fine," she said.

"Found this crew after they ran into some hog lot–type trouble," the Captain told her.

She took a deep breath and looked us over. "Come inside."

• • •

The Mayor's room was almost bare. A mattress, clothes drawers—blankets hung across the room's wide windows as an extra buffer against the cold. The candles lighting the room looked lumpy and bent, like the wax had been melted down and used again.

"You're very lucky to be here right now," the Mayor said.

She told us she had been a nurse outside the city when things stopped working—at the start of the confusion and the fighting. When most people left, she stayed. "That was fifteen, sixteen years ago now?" she added. "Even I tend to lose track." Her skills made her important to the other people still around.

"Hence, after a while, the 'mayor' tag."

The Captain sat slumped in a corner, filing his nails. "Don't let that modesty fool you," he said. "She's a born leader a' men!"

"Keep your nail trimmings off my floor, Carl."

"Case in point!" the Captain chuckled.

There were a few dozen people in the Patchwork Coalition, the Mayor said. "Some families, a few local eccentrics like our Captain here." The big changes had been hardest on the old—there were fewest of them. Anybody was welcome who was willing to help take care of the rest.

"He—the Captain—talked about a 'Pig City,'" I said. "The 'hog lot–trouble.' Who were those men who tried to grab us?"

"Seth Tyson's gang," the Captain said.

"Robbers. And worse," added the Mayor. "A few of them are former residents of our part of town."

The men in the Pig City area raised hogs, the Mayor explained. Fat, pink animals. That was where the smells came from. The men handed the meat off to whatever packs of traders would come through Des Moines. Exchanged it for clothes, medicine, generators for electricity that helped keep the men warm and the meat cold. Seth Tyson was a ruthless trader. His second-in-command, Hank Bradley, was ruthless in everything else.

"Why in a city, though?" Beckley asked. "On our way here, we passed miles of farmland."

"It's an easier place for traders to find, for one thing," the Mayor said. "A big city, near a highway. Until a couple years ago, some of the people that passed through even had gas. *Drove* up. And from what we can tell, Seth's never had a full farm's worth of hogs anyway."

She paused.

"It's more than that, though. It's very . . . convenient for Pig City to be based near the Coalition. They'll steal food of ours, for the pigs, for themselves."

"An' more than that!" the Captain shouted from the corner, his face flushed. Lucas, sitting closer to our group, looked at the ground.

"Seth and the rest will do whatever they have to do to keep those pigs fed. Feed them anything they can get their hands on . . ."

"You don't mean—" Beckley started.

"It started a few seasons ago. Before that, they were just thieves. Violent at worst, but . . . they took a couple of our residents. Young. The kids' parents have moved on. We've stopped a few raids since, but we don't know how many passersby like yourselves they've got. Or how many from the Fellowship."

"Fellowship?"

The Mayor glanced at the Captain and back at us. She looked tired.

"We should be heading to the Civic Center," she said. "It's nearly meeting time. We'll talk while we walk."

"Hold on," I said. "If all this is happening, if it's not going away—why don't you move?"

She sighed, yanking on a heavy coat.

"You probably think it's pride. But it's more than that. To take whole groups of families on the road . . . it'd be harder on the kids, on our older members. We hear reports of disease in Wisconsin, kidnappings in Minnesota . . . It's hard to know where we'd be safer. If there *is* anywhere safer."

# CHAPTER FIVE

"Wait. So you dry most of the food, right? For the winter? You'd have to. That's what I would do. I'm guessing you grind a lot of it down? On the trip here, I tried to make cornmeal, but . . ."

We hardly spoke for most of our walk toward the place the Mayor and the Captain had called the Civic Center. The Mayor's words had shaken me. More than the ambush by the two bald brothers, even. Me, Beckley, Emma—we'd been attacked before. But we'd never felt stuck the way these people were stuck. Just waiting. It took the Captain mentioning soup to start the talking back up. To start Beckley back up, at least.

"And what exactly can you forage for when you get a little outside Des Moines? No. Don't tell me. I'll bet walnuts, currants, leeks . . ."

"She's good!" the Captain said.

"I . . . have a book," Beckley said, turning red in the winter air. "*Gene Matterhorn's Wilderness Survival Guidebook*. Have you heard of it? I think everyone should read it."

Lucas quickened his steps from a few lengths behind Beckley, getting even with her stride. "Um, if you like books, we have a library a few blocks from here. Still plenty of them there. If you want, tomorrow, I could. Um. Take you."

"*What?*" Beckley's eyes glowed behind her cracked glasses. The two of them sped up together as Lucas described the place.

"Heh! Casa-*nova*," the Captain chuckled. He took a step closer to the rest of us. "Now don't any of you get too inquisitive about, er, sanitation matters, by the way, 'less you absolutely have to. Some of that's a per-*pet*-you-uhl source a' contention, if you get my meaning. Disagreements about the, er, surrounding social mores an' the like."

"I don't know what he's saying," whispered Wendell.

• • •

Inside the Civic Center, the Captain shuffled off, mumbling something about making sure someone didn't bungle the soup again. Beckley joined back up with us, staring at her shoes. The quiet boy, Lucas, followed her with his eyes. Wendell opened his mouth, and Beckley shushed him.

"Don't say anything," she said.

"I didn't—"

"Don't. Say. Anything."

He looked at me, and I shrugged.

The cold, sloped floor of the center stretched out in every direction. There were rows and rows of padded seats moving down it, with paths for walking between large columns of them. I didn't know if I'd ever been in a building so big. Our group hung near the edge of a wide, raised area of floor in front of all the chairs. Large boxes with more seats lined the walls near the high ceiling, maybe where people slept. Each footstep I took made an echo.

A few at a time, other people came in. From outside, or from down the steps between rows of seats. Soon a crowd had formed. I counted twenty-five people, twenty-six. Most wore clothes like mine—faded or covered in seams where rips had been stitched back shut. Many of the men wore beards like the Captain. Some were thinner, shorter, had dark skin closer to mine. The women were the same way, different shapes and colors. A few kids, even smaller than Emma, ran around the edge of the crowd as the adults nearby them shook off the cold. A baby poked an arm out from inside one woman's tattered coat. The first time I had seen someone so little since Beckley's mom at the Frontier with Emma.

A few people looked our way, but mostly they kept to each other. Quiet spread through the crowd as the Mayor made her way through, nodding to people or saying a few words. Sometimes she motioned to us, not looking worried, but not waving us over either.

We stayed a few lengths away from the crowd, resting against a stretch of Civic Center wall, as the Mayor went up on the raised floor and started speaking to the whole crowd. She talked about the cold getting worse, there being more snow likely to fall, about people watching their kids and watching out for Pig City men. At that she mentioned us, telling the crowd what she knew about what had happened. Some people nodded and looked over, mostly with soft eyes. I felt apart from them, but welcome, at least.

Soon the Captain and another large man, a dark brow and curly black hair around his ears, brought a big metal container clanging in through a ground-floor doorway. Then a second one. The containers steamed in the Civic Center chill.

"We'll have the group of you stay here tonight," the Mayor said to us. "We can talk

about something more permanent later, if
that's what you choose. There's no heat, as you
can probably tell. But you might find a few
spare mattresses near the balcony seats, and
indoors is indoors."

"Thank you," I said.

"You're welcome to soup, of course," she
continued. "After the day you kids had—"

But the Captain was already headed our
way, a bowl in each hand.

"Onion leek! From one of our latest
forages out," he said. "This one was right
on about the leeks," he added, pointing to
Beckley. I passed the first bowl to Emma, the
second to Wendell. My face felt raw from the
cold, and I paused both times to let steam
from the bowls rise against it.

"While you're here, Carl," the Mayor said,
"why don't you tell the kids about the errand
we discussed."

"Right!" he said. He pointed to Beckley
again, grinning wide. "Well, you're off the
hook, sweetie, in light of, er, yer pending
library visit. The little one too."

Emma scowled.

"You two, though, we're puttin' to work."
Me and Wendell.

"Huh?" Wendell grunted. Soup clung
thick along his top lip.

"Humanitarian aid. A care package. For
the cult down the road," the Captain said.

"Carl!" scolded the Mayor.

"Er, sorry," he said, then mouthed the
word *cult* at us again when she looked away.
Lucas walked over with two more bowls of hot
soup. I grabbed mine so fast some spilled over
the rim and brought the steaming bowl to my
mouth.

# CHAPTER SIX

My back was stiff when I woke the next morning, from the past day's walking and from sleeping with just a couple thin blankets between my body and the hard floor. Wendell grunted in his sleep near the room's opposite wall. I lurched up, wiped the gunk from my eyes, and squinted down from what the Mayor had called a balcony toward the Civic Center floor.

Behind me, a knock sounded on the balcony wall. The Captain held two steaming

bowls in his hands. "Guess what's for break-
*faaast?*" he sang. "Still leek soup.

"Hope you boys don't mind risin' with
the sun," he continued, giving one bowl to
me. "We're running a little behind on winter
preparations, an' I wanna get this out of the
way."

• • •

The snow was up to my ankles when we
stepped outside. It filled in the small cracks
and tears along my boots. I glanced east and
saw the rim of the rising sun.

"That's the way," the Captain said. He
waved toward a bridge past the edge of
Coalition land. As we walked, he explained
about the package Wendell and I were
carrying. About the people he'd called a cult—
the area's third camp.

There weren't many of them, he said—
maybe a dozen. Like the Coalition, they'd
formed sometime after everything fell apart.
Their leader was a man named Arnold Rivers.

"Don't get me wrong, it's not like we've got
lotsa power to go 'round," the Captain said.

"It's cause for celebration anytime one of the generators I've rigged up manages to work. But these folks—after phones, computers, TVs, all those networks 'n' systems crapped out—they took it as a sign."

The Fellowship of Natural Light. They rejected anything electric or engine-powered, said the Captain. Cooked by wood fire, lived by candlelight. It didn't sound that different from a lot of my and Beckley and Emma's life. But we'd have used whatever we could get. The Fellowship lived in a *courthouse*, the Captain said, and refused to live or join with anyone who'd use electricity, like they were to blame for everything falling apart.

"But," the Captain continued, "the Mayor an' some of the others worry about 'em all the same. And we've found that they aren't above a little charity now and again."

The package was filled with nuts, dried currants, and some gloves and blankets the Coalition thought it could spare.

By the time we'd reached the other end of the bridge, the sun was higher. The light shook along the water below us. The Captain unslung his bag and pulled out a fishing pole, bent and taped together in some places.

"Drop-off point's about two blocks farther," he said. "You boys wanna do the honors? Don't take the extra block to the courthouse itself. They won't like it." He grinned. "I'll keep watch near the bridge. And see if I can find somethin' for dinner besides leek soup. River's not frozen over yet. Any trouble, just shout. I've got a baseball bat too."

Wendell and I stepped off the bridge and walked onward through the snow.

"That guy's weird," he said.

"I kinda like him," I said.

"What does electricity do?"

"It—uh, I'll have Beckley explain it."

"I like that soup."

"Mm-hmm."

"The leek soup."

"I know the one, Wendell."

"You think the weird guy would show me how to make the soup?"

We moved through the first block, more wide buildings with lots of windows. Then Wendell stopped. My arm jerked back, still gripping my side of the package.

"Malik. Listen," he murmured. "Footsteps. I can hear 'em."

I stopped too and circled around. Nothing.

"Maybe it's one of those Fellowship people," I said. "Or maybe just the wind."

At that a gust cut through the cross street in front of us. Snow swooped off the ground. Wendell whipped his head back in the direction we'd walked. Nothing there either. He frowned.

"Let's keep going," I said. "Slowly. I've got my pocketknife, if we need it."

I tried to keep my breaths slow, but my heart beat faster and faster. My mind moved to a lesson from the Matterhorn guide that I'd used to practice reading. If you think a cougar might be in your area, make noise—you don't want to surprise it. If one sees you, freeze— you don't want to trigger a chase response. Then back away slow.

On hills and plains, the book was a lot more useful. No lessons in it about cities, or defense against people.

The winds hit us as we stepped into the intersection, the chill snaking through my clothes. Halfway down the block, a metal trashcan banged against the ground, rolling. Behind it, a young boy with black hair stood up. Not one we'd seen at the Coalition meeting. He looked at us with scared eyes, wide, with dark rings around them.

I called over, "It's all right—"

But he was already running. Almost as soon as he'd started, he tripped moving across a curb. The little boy's chin landed on the concrete underneath the snow.

I told Wendell to wait with the package.

"But we're not supposed to—"

The boy started to pick himself up, shaky.

"He looks hurt," I said. "And he doesn't know us, why we're here. If he runs back with blood on his face talking about people from over the bridge—I just wanna talk to him, so people don't get the wrong idea."

By that time I was walking. Wendell sat
down on top the package, glancing back and
forth. Before I reached the little boy, he was
running again.

"Wait!" I shouted. "It's okay!"
He headed down the cross street away
from the intersection—and away from
the courthouse we'd been heading toward.
Running scared, not thinking where he was
headed.

I rushed past the spot where the boy fell,
and my feet slid in different directions on the
ice beneath the snow. I looked up to see the boy
dashing farther down the street. I scrambled
back up after him, shaking my head.

*Dumb*, I thought. *If he wasn't scared
before* . . .

I caught up a few blocks later and slowed
my run. Gently, I set a hand on the boy's
shoulder. Still shaking, he stopped. Blood
curved along his chin and tears lined his eyes.

"Kid," I said. "Really, it's okay. I'm here to
give you and your family some food. Sorry if I
scared you. My name's Malik. What's yours?"

While I spoke, the little boy's eyes shifted to something behind me. He started breathing fast and said nothing. I squinted down the path we'd taken—in the distance, Wendell was nowhere to be seen. By that time I could hear breathing behind me too, footsteps that the snow had muffled 'til then. The boy cried out and covered his eyes, and then everything went black.

# CHAPTER SEVEN

*I* woke for the second time that morning, curled up inside a cage. A fence made of thin strands of metal held me in on every side. Next to me was the little kid who fell in the snow. He crouched, shivering, one cage over, his arms wrapped around his shins.

It might've been the smell that woke me. It was worse than ever. The stink seemed to fill my mouth. The cages were indoors, part of a much larger room. Thin bands of sunlight lit the place, filtering in from slats near the ceiling.

Below me was a platform—a grate—and then a long, four-sided open floor. Up and down the floor were metal tables, stained with rust or blood. Along the wall, all sorts of tools I'd never seen before. Noises floated in from a hallway that started at one corner of the wall opposite our cages—grunts, not human. This was Pig City.

I turned again to the shivering boy. "Don't be scared. We're going to get out of here. I'm Malik."

The boy started to back away from me inside his cage, then paused. "I'm Abner."

"Does your family live in a courthouse, Abner?"

He nodded.

"Well, we're gonna get you right back there."

The lock on my cage was small, a thin metal loop that fit into a small gold-colored box. I patted my pants, feeling around for my knife. Gone. No way to pick the lock. And no breaking it.

My stomach trembled. It had already burned through the soup. I squinted back toward the sunlight coming through near the ceiling—and felt a drop of water hit my head. Above me was Wendell, soaked from melted snow, climbing across two long, high pipes. Shadows kept him tucked out of sight.

"Malik!" he hissed. "I followed you!"

I motioned for the little boy to be silent, and he nodded.

"Anyone see you, Wendell?"

He shook his head no.

"One of those tools, by the tables. If you get one, think you can bust us out?"

"Yeah," he whispered back.

Wendell began to shuffle down from the pipes, and a door slammed somewhere below the bottom of my cage.

"Up!" I mouthed to Wendell. "Up, up!"

Footsteps echoed on the floor of the room. Then up the metal steps to our cages. More drops of water landed on my head, and I tried to wipe it dry.

One of the bald brothers lumbered along the grate in front of the cages. Next to him was a stub-nosed shorter man, thick square glasses, a brown beard with silver streaks, cut closer than the Captain's. His hair looked wet, pressed back against his skull. In one hand, he held a black pole with two short prongs at its end.

"Here's the two of 'em, Hank!" the bald man said. "Me and Duane caught 'em. I think the little one's from over in the courthouse. This guy here's the one we caught the other day."

He pointed to me.

"Thanks," the other man said. His voice was froggy and mean. He looked to Daryll. "That'll be all."

As the big bald man clanged off, Hank Bradley looked me over.

"Where you from, kid?"

I said nothing. Talking could only help them, I decided.

"Many more come here with you?"

Nothing again. The man nodded at me and then stepped to Abner's cage. He touched the pronged black stick between the bars of the cage, and it gave off a shrill electric buzz. He shook the stick back and forth, bellowing at the boy. Abner ran to the back and covered his head.

The man laughed a quiet laugh. "You're"—he cleared his throat—"*not*-speaking for the both of you. Get me? Let's try this again."

I heard another drop hit the floor behind me. Maybe the shadows hid the water falling off of Wendell. But sunlight was creeping slowly back into the cages. I dragged the wet bottoms of my shoes squeaking against the grate beneath me to cover the dripping noise.

Hank Bradley tucked his glasses into the pocket of a checkered shirt underneath his tan jacket. From another pocket, he drew a set of keys. He moved to Abner's cage but looked at me.

"Alright," he said. "I can wait, but I bet the pigs can't."

"Hold on!" I shouted.

"He can talk!" he shouted in reply. He shoved the keys back in his pocket. "*Now!* Where. Are. You. From?"

I opened my mouth again, but before I could speak I heard a sound I'd never heard before. From Hank Bradley's jacket. Like a bird squawk inside a tin can.

"Hank!" Another man's voice, high and shrill. Also coming from inside the jacket?

Hank Bradley pulled out something small, boxy, and black, with a pole on top.

"Mr. Tyson."

"Your status?"

"With the two that Duane and Daryll picked up. One of 'em's Fellowship. The other's . . . somethin' else. If he's Coalition, it's not somebody I recognize. I've been working on getting his story." He looked at me. "Started to."

The squawk sounded again.

"That can wait," the voice said. "Right now we need you on the floor. Half the men are likely to try putting down a pig and bump off each other by mistake."

"Sir, I've got a gut feelin'—"

"It can wait. Remember—this week we've got to increase production. Get on the floor, and from there, make sure the men are in raiding shape."

"Yessir."

The talking box squawked off.

"I'm not finished with you kids. Not nearly." Hank Bradley turned and stomped down the metal grate. The door underneath me slammed shut again.

"Okay. Malik," Wendell whispered, "I'm coming d—"

He slid from the pipes and landed hard on top of my cage, making a bump in the fencing. The sides rattled, and I ground my teeth. From his corner, Abner looked up in confusion.

Wendell scanned the room, not moving, then climbed down one side of my cage after hearing no noise.

"Wait," he whispered. He came back a moment later with a tool from the wall. It was wide, rectangle-shaped, but it looked sharp on one end. Sunlight flickered off the tool when Wendell raised it by its handle. The snapped locks fell to the ground.

I held my hand out to Abner. He didn't move.

I thought about the Frontier Motel for a moment—how scary the rest of the world had seemed when I was smaller, when I'd only known a little of it. And it must have been worse for Abner. He had been *raised* to be afraid.

"Anything that can happen to you getting out of this place," I pleaded, "cannot be as bad as what will happen if you stay."

When that didn't work, I carried him. I propped him up just outside the cage, and he obeyed.

At the bottom of the steps away from the cages, I looked across the room. Besides the opening to the hall that pig noises traveled in from, there were two doorways. One underneath the cages. One with double doors, no windows. And a thin puddle of mud and water at the foot of it. I nodded at the windowless doors, turning to Wendell.

"Outside's good, right?"

"It's how I got in."

"Alright," I sighed. "Alright."

# CHAPTER EIGHT

Soon as we stepped outside, Wendell thought he heard people coming. And he'd been right before. Not wanting to risk Hank Bradley coming back, we nudged open the door of a building across from us.

It was a cold I'd never felt before. Frost lined the walls around us. My throat tensed up, and the freeze crept into my veins. Icy hunks of red and pink meat hung from hooks and chains on the ceiling.

I waved to Wendell and Abner. "Let's get

to the back. Behind the pigs."

A steady hum filled the room, from whatever kept the air so cold. As we walked deeper inside, I noticed the room blocked out most of the smell, too.

"How long do we wait?" Wendell asked.

"I dunno," I said. "If they're putting down pigs somewhere else, it can't be that long 'til someone comes in."

Hot breaths drifted out in front of me. Wendell picked at the side of a pig and put flecks of the meat in his mouth, cringing sometimes from the frost left on. I shoved my hands far into my coat pockets, my fingers stiff and raw.

"Whoever you heard," I whispered to Wendell, "they're probably gone. Maybe not far, but gone."

He nodded and shuddered from the cold.

Holding one of the little boy's hands with mine, I stepped back toward the front. After wrapping the other hand in my sleeve, I slowly twisted the door handle. Wendell slid his head near mine. Through the opening, we heard small voices—faraway yelling. Then nothing.

"Maybe they went the other way," Wendell whispered.

"Then we leave," I said. "Now."

As we stepped out of the freezing building, a man turned the corner to our right. He was thin and small, shrunken-looking like a dried fruit. White and blond hair came to a point high on his forehead. Light footsteps.

At first the man's eyes were fixed on the ground. He murmured, "incompetent . . . do not have the time for this," in the same high voice that we'd heard on Hank Bradley's speaking machine. Seth Tyson. He tilted his head up and stopped, and so did we. Understanding twisted up his face.

"Hhhaaaank!" he shrieked into his own speaking machine.

We ran the other way as Mr. Tyson's machine squawked on, hearing only the rough shape of his angry shouts.

• • •

Pig City was a maze of sheds and garages and other boxy buildings. Sometimes, in the gaps between them, I saw the first building we'd run out of—a big warehouse in the center of things. But there was no telling which path out was the safest or the shortest run back to the Coalition.

The pig stink got worse as I tore down a path where muddy footprints smudged out the snow. Abner coughed and kept his head down, still clutching my hand. Behind us, Wendell tripped and caught himself, glancing back every few steps to see if anyone was chasing us.

"Keep going!" he wheezed. "Those big guys, the one with the beard, more! Running—two blocks back!"

But a fence stopped me right then—slats of nailed-together wood below my knees. Before I could halt my run, my shin smashed through the rotting fence boards. Abner and I landed in a mess of mud, pig slop, and gnawed-over bones.

Pigs squealed and scampered around the pen's edges. One whined "rheeeee!" into my ear, and I swung to smack it away, slipping in the mud, dropping back down on my back.

"Go go go go go go!" shouted Wendell. He tapped at my shoulder, frantic, dragging Abner by the arm. I spat out wet dirt and looked around in a blur. The animals looked fierce, but they were panicked. They collided with each other in the filth near the pen's edges. I lost my footing again, and Wendell grabbed me. As I started to run forward, I felt a crunch under my boot, something brittle caving in like the bones of a rib cage.

We'd crawled over the back of a fat, black-spotted hog and past the fence on the other side by the time Tyson's men had reached the pen. A few of them linked arms and stepped in front of holes in the broken fence. A couple pigs tried squeezing through the men's legs.

"Don't let those pigs get loose!" Hank Bradley yelled. "Do *not!*"

For just a moment I stopped, Wendell and Abner well out of the pen in front of me. Then I kicked down a stretch of fence on the side nearest us and started running again.

# CHAPTER NINE

*I*'d barely had time to change out of my mud-covered clothes before the Mayor came calling at the Civic Center.

"After you were back outside of Pig City . . . what did you do?" she asked.

"We took the kid—Abner—over to the courthouse," I said. "After all that, we weren't gonna leave him anywhere but home. I don't know what happened to the package."

For the first time, I saw a smile move

across the Mayor's face. She nodded, like the lost package was okay.

"I . . . spoke to them. More of them," I added.

"Members of the Fellowship?" The smile left her. "What did they say?"

"They didn't want to say anything, seemed like. The skinny guy with beady eyes, Rivers. The rest of the grown-ups. I think they only heard me out 'cause I'd kept the kid safe. I told them that they can't expect to live the way they live for a lot longer. It's not safe. They said thank you, but they didn't let me say any more. All of 'em went inside."

The Mayor sighed. "They've heard that before."

My voice got shaky as I kept going. I tried to explain it right. "No—it's more than that. When we were in Pig City . . . I think they're planning something big. We heard stuff about raiding. About 'increasing production.'"

For a moment, the Mayor was very still. Then she got up, said thank you, and walked fast out of the room.

• • •

From a high spot in the Civic Center, Wendell and I saw Beckley and Emma moving down a column of seats. The boy our age, Lucas, was with them. He and Beckley walked close together as Emma ran toward us.

"Malik! Wendell! Are you okay?" Beckley asked. "We heard you were in Pig City! What happened?"

"Cages. Pig slop," I groaned. "Can we talk about it later?"

"Pig City is gross," added Wendell.

"I'm so glad you guys are okay!" Beckley said. She paused. "You *are* okay?"

We nodded.

"Okay," she continued, "because there are some *amazing* things at that library."

I pushed off my boots and sat up against a wall.

"I learned so many *words* today!" Beckley said. "I tried writing them all down, but it got to be too many." She pulled out a sheet of paper with scratches of her handwriting, one edge rough and torn.

"It's an end sheet, so Lucas said it was

okay," she whispered to us, and then smiled at him. "Guess how many words I can use just to talk about that man the Captain? You could say he's *heavyset*. Or *rotund*. Also *gregarious*!"

"You looked at words all day?" asked Wendell.

"We, uh, got sort of sidetracked a couple times," Lucas said softly, his eyes hidden behind his thick glasses and brown hair.

"Quiet, you," Beckley replied, tapping his ankle with the tip of her boot. "Oh, and Lucas told me about this thing called science fiction? It's in books. It sounds *so* good."

"What's that?" Wendell said.

"It's sort of like, um—uh, you know what, I'll explain it later."

"Can you explain about electricity?" Wendell added.

Beckley kept going. "There's this book called *Cat's Cradle*, and Lucas says it's about the end of the world. But not the way the world really ended, or there'd be ice all over the place. What I mean is . . ."

• • •

Later, at dinner, Emma drank soup with us on the Civic Center floor. Her sister sat nearby, talking and talking to Lucas.

"They act like a mom and dad," Emma said to Wendell and yanked on a tangle of hair.

Wendell looked to me to explain, and I shook my head. I was not tackling it.

"Yep!" Wendell chirped. "Weird!"

The Captain had been passing out soup since the start of the meal. He hadn't looked our way. But once he'd poured the last bowl, he circled his way to me and Wendell. He gripped his hat with both hands.

"Boys"—he peeked up at us—"boys, I—gah, I'm so embarrassed. I should've—I'm so, so sorry. It was dumb, dumb, dumb. I'm so glad you two aren't hurt. I wish I coulda—"

"No fish?" I asked.

He looked at me, blank, then breathed out a heavy breath. His chuckles got louder, a little at a time.

"No fish," he laughed. "Sorry 'bout that too."

He put a big hand on top of Emma's hair and messed it up.

"You kids wanna see something?"

• • •

The Captain's room wasn't in a tall building like most other people's. He kept a small garage to himself, a couple blocks from the Civic Center. His bed lay in a corner, surrounded by tools and machine parts all along the ground.

"Watch your step!" he shouted, like a joke. "Now—normally I don't bring the stereo out, 'cept for special occasions. Gets exhausting, as you'll see. But . . . an apology's as much an occasion as anything, I suppose. And anyway, now I'm entertaining guests!"

The Captain held up something shiny and circle-shaped. Then he put the shiny circle in the top of some machine, round and purple and gray. A bundle of wires stuck out from the back of the machine, some thick and black, some thin and red or yellow. Patches of tape held them on. The wires fed into a small black box, and more wires stuck out the box's back end. Those wires stopped at a flat, palm-sized board covered in rows of switches and attached to what looked like a handle. The Captain flipped a switch and started turning the hand crank.

"Mister Bob Seger!" the Captain yelled. "Fer what I'm guessing is the first time in yer young lives. *Rock and Roll Never Forgets!*"

The sounds coming from the gray and purple machine sounded like people banging together bits of metal. Like, in a pattern. Too many noises at once—hard to separate one from the others. In the middle of it, from nowhere, a man started screaming. I pictured a tiny person trapped inside the machine.

"What *is* this?" Wendell whispered to me, or tried to, hissing above the noise. "I *hate this.*"

The Captain turned red and squeezed his hat again. He switched the machine off with his other hand. "It's, erm, not fer everybody. Anyway, we're here for bigger things."

He trotted to the other side of the garage and pulled a big cloth off the top of what looked like another big cloth.

"Tah-dah!" he said. "If you ever wondered why they call me the Captain . . ."

Wendell shook his head no.

"Kid, you're a freakin' handful," the Captain murmured. "This right here. This! Is my personal hot air balloon . . . er, in progress."

"Uh. What's it do?" I asked.

"Holy moley, this really will be an education for you kids. It's a flying machine!"

He dragged over a large, pieced-together crate, big enough for a few people to stand in.

"This here's the basket," the Captain continued. "Wicker, aluminum—I can't afford to be too picky."

He grabbed a pinch of the big sheet on the ground and started shaking it up and down. Closer up, it looked like a giant sleeping bag.

"An' this here's the balloon itself. The *envelope*, we call it. Fill this thing with heated-up air and *whoosh*! You're sailing."

"Can we fly in it?" asked Emma.

"That's, er, the in-progress part," the Captain said. "It's flight-ready, I'm convinced. I've got all the component parts . . . save fer a propane burner. That, the Pig City boys stole a while back, to properly light their farts with and the like."

His shoulders dropped, but I caught a gleam in his eye. "But lemme tell you kids something: when this thing gets up, it's gonna be something incredible."

# CHAPTER TEN

By the time we'd gone back to the Civic Center, it had emptied out again. Beckley sat in one of the seats midway up the floor, a book in one hand and a candle in the other.

"Emma!" she shouted. "It's time for *you* to get to bed."

Emma stomped up the steps toward the sleeping rooms. Wendell followed, yawning. I had started to go too when Beckley set her book down.

"Wait," she said. "Let's talk."

We began to walk around the floor and between the rows of padded seats, Beckley lighting the way with her candle.

"Now, I know I'm not the one who got knocked out and shoved in a cage today, but—I think we were right to come here."

"That's at least half true," I said.

"I'm serious!" Beckley replied. "It's . . . nice. We've never seen this before! All these people, using the tools they have, working together . . ."

"And that boy, huh?"

Her face turned red in the candlelight.

"Lucas? He's . . . sweet. He seems very sweet. 'And that boy.'" She paused. "I think we should think about staying."

"Beckley, we haven't been here two days."

"I know, Malik! I'm just saying, we should think about it. You suggested it anyway, at first, right? Sort of."

I ground my teeth. "We don't know how much time we have. That's the thing. These people, they're in danger. More than they know. The Pig City people . . . I think they're about to do something bad."

We both said nothing for a few steps.

"But . . . we at least stay and help the fight, right?" Beckley asked.

"Yeah," I said. "Yeah, I think we owe them that."

As we completed the loop, Beckley blew lightly on the flame, watching it wave and tremble.

"And right now . . . do we stand guard? Can we sleep?"

"Why don't you stand guard?" I said. "I got knocked out and thrown in a cage this morning."

• • •

People gathered again in the Civic Center at the start of the next day. Beckley woke up in the chair where she'd been keeping watch and got the rest of us.

"The Mayor's talking," she said. "Looks serious."

In the area people called the *pit*, a few kids yawned and rubbed at their eyes, awake earlier than usual. The men and women bunched together like crows perched in a tree—legs fixed, but bodies twitching, heads hung or snapping back and forth. The baby of a woman near the outside of the crowd started to waah, and the mother wrapped her scarf around it. The Mayor's words to the crowd were flat, her voice faded and rough, like an echo of itself. The man we'd seen standing guard the first day was next to her.

"Mitch has posted lookouts on every door outside the Center," the Mayor said. "I'd ask that no one leave here unless you have to. If you do, clear it with one of the men at the doors. Any concern about valuables, please keep it to a minimum. It's human life we're thinking about here. The rest we can rebuild.

"This could be nothing," she continued, "but I'd prefer not to take that chance. Rumors of a Pig City raid are something we'll continue to take seriously. After two nights, we'll reassess the situation."

I looked around for the Captain but couldn't see him. Probably standing guard outside.

Emma dragged her feet along a chewed-up strip of carpet. "Do we just have to stay here?"

"*Yes*," said Beckley.

"You still got your bola?" I asked her.

Beckley nodded. "You still got your knife?"

I shook my head. "Lost it. Pig City."

The rest of that morning, we waited. Wendell and Emma fell back asleep without meaning to. Beckley holed up with the book Lucas had given her. I walked around, thinking of ways to make another weapon, partly just to pass the time. Checking the ground for nails or loose screws. I was scared, restless, and trying to hold on to each peaceful moment.

# CHAPTER ELEVEN

*I* found the Captain posted outside a pair of
double doors near the start of the afternoon.
The sun hung half-hidden behind clouds,
and the Captain's face poked out from a scarf
wrapped snug under his nose.

"Does it get like this a lot?" I asked.

"No," the Captain said with a sniff.
"Nah. Plenty a' times, people've all gathered
together, after a raid or someone going
missing. But never quite like this."

I took a step out onto Locust Avenue

and looked far up and down the street. No movement, not even snow dropping off ledges in the weak sunlight.

"We're not . . ." the Captain continued, "we're not dreamers, ya know? Not out to build the sorta society we always wanted, nothin' that big-minded. A person like the Mayor's gotta be strong for everybody. But even her, I dunno if she thinks this can last forever. What you said 'bout what you heard in Pig City—maybe she's been 'specting to hear something like that for a while."

He spun the head of his baseball bat against the ground. "I think ya spooked her."

The sun slid farther behind the clouds after I crouched down near the Captain, keeping watch. He'd shoved his bag to one side and picked up a metal rectangle half as big as the door it leaned against. Then he handed the big piece of metal to me.

"Baking sheet. Industrial size," he said. Noticing my confusion, he added, "Fer protection."

Seeing Abner stepping carefully down the

street, like something from a dream, got me to my feet. Two other kids, also pale and dark-haired, his age, walked behind him.

I ran to them but didn't know whether to send the kids back across the bridge or to rush them inside the Civic Center.

"It's *not* safe for you out here!" I yelped. "Abner, what are you . . . ?"

He looked down at his feet, and his chin trembled. "I wanted to tell you thank you," he said quietly. "Dad says not to talk to people outside the Fellowship, but he also says to be grateful to those who show kindness to others."

Without looking up, Abner reached into his coat pocket, then handed me a brown glass bottle. It was covered with white blurs around the middle of it, where paper had been ripped off.

"It's from my collection," he said, still quiet. "I find them."

"Abner, that is very nice of you, but listen—"

"Abner, I'm scared," one of the others whispered. A girl, wide-eyed, with hair in two black braids.

"You said you wanted to join my adventure," Abner whispered back. "You always ask to go on my explorings."

"Yes, but now we are scared," said the third child, another boy.

"Fer cryin' out loud, this is a nightmare," the Captain said behind me, muzzling a yell. "Now? Of course this would hafta happen right now," he murmured.

He turned to me. "I'm gonna get these kids inside and get the Mayor, an' then have a heart attack if I can find the time. You stay on guard."

The Captain shuffled the shivering kids into the building while I nodded to Abner that it was okay to go along with him. I stayed outside, rubbing my arms and staring at the bottle by my feet.

Not long after the Captain went in with Abner and the others, I saw a man walking the same path the kids had taken. Like them, he was dark-haired and pale. Tall and thin, wearing dark clothes and no coat, he moved through the snow in uneven steps.

Up close, the man's face was sharp and narrow. His eyes were small. He shook as he stepped toward me, from the cold or from anger. It was the same man Wendell and I had spoken to when we returned Abner.

"Where are the children?" he shouted. "I want to see them right away!"

He gasped for breath, then squinted at me. "You. I recognize you. You're the one responsible for this. Endangering my son, and now tempting him and the others to risk their safety . . ."

"I kept your kid from being pig food," I said. "Also—can I ask why he collects bottles?"

"At ease, Malik," the Mayor said flatly as the doors clicked open behind me. The Captain followed.

"The children are fine, Arnold. They're inside. You're welcome to join them. It might be safer than the walk back, for the time being."

"Absolutely not. We've tolerated your overtures for long enough, but this is unacceptable. I'm taking the children, and—"

"*Which you are welcome to do,*" the Mayor said. She rubbed her forehead. "But listen: this is a *bad* time to be out. We've had warnings of raids from the pig camp—"

"Which would be a fitting judgment, I think," Arnold Rivers from the Fellowship replied.

"Want me to get the kids? I'll get the kids," the Captain snapped, then murmured something about Rivers needing vitamin C.

We first heard glass breaking to the west of the Civic Center. The crash of cracked windows, past the big, bent-looking piece of public art. Running into the street, I saw small shards fly into the open air from a couple stories up. Again and again, only blocks away, glass dropping like snowflakes. The Pig City men had arrived, running through home after home.

For a few moments we all stood still, listening to the glass burst. Then the thin man from the Fellowship spoke with a small voice. "We will stay, if you'll permit us, until the men have taken what they want."

"They've got pigs to feed," the Mayor said, just as small. "They aren't looking for warm coats or water filters. They want bodies."

# CHAPTER TWELVE

The men who'd smashed up the Coalition living spaces kept their distance at first. I saw a couple of them rush out the front of the tall buildings—not worrying about being seen, after all the noise. Neither approached the Civic Center. But one man stayed put for a moment as the other moved back, looking our way and talking on a talking machine like I'd seen in Pig City.

Arnold Rivers from the Fellowship slunk inside the Civic Center, and I gripped my baking sheet tight, staying by the double doors.

"People are gonna need you inside, Catherine," the Captain said to the Mayor. "We're all right here."

As she turned back through the doors, the Captain squinted down the path where Pig City men had busted the windows. "Can't be all of it. They've gotta have more for us," he murmured, mostly to himself. "Hollld steady, hollllld steady."

He was right. And we didn't have to wait long.

The Captain's breathing started to get faster, and he kept on murmuring to himself. "There's enough of us. Just hollld steady." Repeating those words even as we began to see men from Pig City between buildings around the center. What had to be nearly all of them, planted on each street that boxed in the Civic Center. Some of them carried sticks like the one Hank Bradley had shown me and Abner, the kind that set off a jolt. A few of them, moving in pairs, had brought over what looked like cages, the kind I'd been locked in, two long metal bars underneath for carrying whoever they meant to capture.

On a corner on Locust Avenue, I saw Hank Bradley himself. He barked at a cluster of men holding cloth pouches sagging with fist-sized bulges. Slings.

Bradley walked throughout the cluster, man by man, setting fire to the loads inside each sling. And one by one, the men started darting toward us, a few running steps, and letting the flaming loads loose.

Streaks of fire drifted over our heads, to one side or another. The flames started as the men began refilling their slings. I held the baking sheet up above my head, tensing my arms and stealing short looks out onto the streets.

"You keep that thing right in front of you, Malik!" the Captain shouted.

The sound of breaking glass splintered over whatever he shouted next. Louder, nearer to us. As the slingshot loads smashed through the windows into the Civic Center, the Captain and I looked to each other, wide-eyed.

The men from Pig City stepped closer on every side I could see. The smell of smoke started to mix with the downwind stink of pigs. Somewhere close, more glass broke.

Mitch, the leader of the guard, banged through our double doors from inside. I stared in and saw the Mayor behind him, urging a pack of kids and their mother to stay calm, stay together.

"Mitch, Catherine!" the Captain bellowed. "It's not safe out here! They're bustin' in!"

In the open doorway, the smell of smoke got stronger. Behind the Mayor, fire crackled.

"We need to regroup!" the Mayor replied. "They don't want inside—they want us out here!"

Mitch and the Captain kept the kids together while the Mayor ducked back in the building. She came out again a moment later, leading another family through the doors. By that time, the sound of fire inside had risen to a roar.

Wendell came around a corner, coughing, Beckley and Emma behind him. Other people, faces I half-recognized from mealtimes, followed them.

"Is that everyone?" Mitch shouted.

The Mayor heaved. "Should be! When we left, we saw the others through back exits!"

"Where's Lucas?" the Captain shouted to Beckley.

"He grabbed a cart and ran off," she said. "He wouldn't listen when we said stay—he said he had to get something for you!"

At that the Captain tore the hat off his head, shooting looks left and right. "Ah jeez, Idea Man's gone insane. Ah jeez." He took a few unsure steps that turned into a run. "I'll be back!" he shouted.

The Mayor, Mitch, and a few other grown-ups tried to keep people together. They shouted at two crowds at once to form two lines, telling people nearby to grab hands. But black smoke began drifting from every opening of the Civic Center, and panic spread like flame. People ran in different directions, screaming out for family or slipping in the snow. And then the men from Pig City were on us.

I ran to the edge of the mess of Coalition members, meeting the men as they closed in. My baking sheet clanged against fists and heads and chains. The skin on my knuckles kept splitting, and my gloves got damp. I kicked and huffed and swung the sheet—a dozen times or a hundred, I couldn't tell. Sometimes my eye would catch Beckley's bola circling through the air.

As the fight went on, I saw fewer Pig City men standing. A couple ran, bloodied, a couple lay on the ground. I wondered, in a blur, if our numbers had made a difference.

The baking sheet shook in my hand as a red-haired, hard-eyed man brought one of the jolting sticks down against it. The shock traveled through the metal sheet, my gloves saving my hands.

"Malik!" Wendell yelled from somewhere. "Watch out!"

I swung left in time to see another man, a tall bald twin, move at me with another jolting stick. I blocked him, too, and then felt a shock move through my body from the back of my neck. Numb before I hit the ground.

The next moments were more a blur than before.

I saw pairs of feet I couldn't tell apart.

Couldn't move.

Heard shouts that I couldn't make out.

Except Wendell's.

His voice grew louder, 'til it was like he was above me. Shaky, strained, and fierce.

"Stay away! *Stay away!* I won't let you hurt *Maliiik!*"

And then a crack like thunder split the air. And silence.

I watched Wendell hit the ground next to me, his blood start to glide my way and then melt the snow beneath it.

Then Seth Tyson spoke: "Stay where you are, Catherine. I'm reloading."

# CHAPTER THIRTEEN

Anger brought the blur of noise and movement around me into focus. Everything was sharp, clear: the old scar on Wendell's face, the color fading from his skin, the steam where his blood touched the snow. My arms and legs had been numb from the jolt to my neck, but they started to shake. Somewhere near me, Seth Tyson cawed orders at the Mayor.

"Very considerate, to gather everyone in one place like this," he said, his voice high. "You must've known we were coming. Now

I probably don't have to tell you we're on sort of a timetable. Traders are coming all the way from Chicago, any day now, and we need our pigs plump!"

Slowly, I dragged my arms underneath my chest, lifting my head off the ground. Looking to Wendell, I ran through a dozen things I maybe could have done different to keep him from lying there, lifeless.

Seth Tyson kept talking while the Mayor said nothing. "These next moments are crucial, Catherine. How much you cooperate could determine how . . . gracious we'll be. Who knows? We might not even need *all* of you. A few of you we could keep around to shovel the pig slop."

His voice got quieter, less relaxed. "The cages we brought over. Tell your people to get in them."

I cocked my head to see the Mayor spit a mess of blood in the snow. Tyson pointed his gun toward the sky—a gun! We'd never seen one up close—and the sound of thunder filled the air again.

"Do it!" Tyson shrieked. The Mayor stayed silent and turned partway toward the crowd around her. Tyson's first shot had frozen most people in place. A handful of Coalition men held their grips on Pig City men. A handful of Pig City men held their grips on Coalition types. All of them waited on the Mayor's next word.

She raised her shoulders and shouted, far into the crowd, "Run, if you can! Protect yourselves, your families! If you can go, *go*!"

A few people at a time, the crowd moved away and toward the Civic Center, but slowly, maybe to not set off Seth Tyson. Tyson fidgeted with a small box until he pulled out two more large rounds. He cracked the gun open at a joint past its handle.

"Was that really asking for too much?" he asked, half to himself, and reloaded.

The Mayor tensed up, not running herself. As Tyson's gun clicked back shut, the Captain's booming voice began to echo off the walls of buildings nearby. His hot air balloon passed overhead through the black smoke of the Civic Center. The Captain and Lucas clung to opposite walls of the basket while the balloon swung from side to side, shaky and drifting downward.

*The burner*, I thought. *Lucas ran to steal a burner.*

"What in God's name is that?" Tyson murmured, mouth wide open. He began yelling for Hank Bradley. Meanwhile the Captain bellowed at the heads of Coalition types below: "Round up the kids! As many as you can, we can take 'em!"

I hadn't asked the Captain how far the balloon could go, but right then anywhere would have been better than Des Moines. A pack of four or five, then six or seven, kids formed as the scene started to unfreeze. Coalition grown-ups pushed at Pig City men to keep away, Arnold Rivers too. I thought I saw the bottom of the basket sag and wondered how much it could hold.

Seth Tyson aimed his gun past the Mayor toward the balloon. He thundered a shot off, and it disappeared into the Civic Center flames as the balloon spun and swerved.

"Back up, back up!" the Captain shouted at Lucas. "Evasive maneuvers! No no no—"

I shoved myself the rest of the way off the ground, still weak. Lucas seemed to panic at the balloon's controls as the basket headed closer to me, the Mayor, and Tyson's gun. Waiting patiently for the Captain and Lucas to cross his path, Hank Bradley launched a flaming load from his sling clean through the balloon's puffy envelope. The balloon started sinking fast, taking sharp turns in the air like a snake. I lunged for Tyson as he raised his gun again.

With Tyson scrawny and losing his calm, and me worn down by the jolt, we were a match. I grabbed at his gun with both arms, and another shot went up into the air. Empty. It slid from his grip as we tumbled into the snow. He planted his knees onto my chest, tore off his gloves, and scratched at my face with wiry arms, swipe after swipe of stinging cuts. I heaved up, flipping on top of him, in time to see Beckley's bola dent a cluster of Pig City men who stood in the balloon's wild path.

The Captain and Lucas held tight to the flaming balloon's edges as it sped toward us, four men high, then three, then two. And— "Nnnnaah!"—Seth Tyson wriggled a leg free and connected with my jaw. I blinked hard, teeth clamping, and saw the Captain's foot burst through the bottom of the basket. He barked a curse before the balloon was on top of us. I pushed Tyson to the ground and shut my eyes to the sound of the basket's supports snapping above my head.

# CHAPTER FOURTEEN

The first thing I saw when I opened my eyes was Lucas on top of the Captain on top of Seth Tyson. A few lengths away lay the hot air balloon, basket smashed and a wide hole burned in the limp fabric of the envelope. The burner rolled in the snow, wheezing gas.

A hand clamped on my shoulder, and I looked up to see the Mayor. She'd pulled me clear of the crash.

"Captain!" she shouted. "Lucas!"

Lucas stirred at the top of the pile and slid

off. The Captain, eyes closed, stayed put and mumbled, "Gonna be a minute." Tyson kept still, crumpled up and knocked out beneath the big man.

"It flies!" the Captain added.

The Mayor turned back to me. "You okay?"

I nodded. "Think so."

Struggling to stand, I scanned the streets in front of me. The fight had ended with the crash. A few faces I couldn't find—Hank Bradley, one of the big bald twins. Maybe they had run. But most Pig City men lay bound up or caged. Snow had started to fall again, but the fire inside the Civic Center raged. Snowflakes disappeared into the flames.

The Mayor straightened up and turned to Mitch and a few other grown-ups. "If you can, help Lucas prop up the Captain," she said. "I have to start looking at the wounded. Let's lead Mr. Tyson to one of those cages." Her eyes fell on Wendell. Then she met my stare. "I'm sorry about your friend. He was very brave."

From behind the crowd, Emma began bounding toward me, then stopped, held back by her sister. Beckley placed a hand over her mouth, eyes wide through her cracked glasses. She looked to Wendell on the ground and then to me. I nodded, grim, and Beckley started to tremble. I took my jacket off and set it across the body. An ache pulled tight in me, and I felt trapped by the smells of blood, smoke, and pig stink.

## CHAPTER FIFTEEN

The Pig City men who ran must have kept running. Des Moines was quiet in the days after the fight. And Pig City stayed empty, except for the pigs.

The men who got captured were treated for their wounds—after everyone else was. The Mayor said Seth Tyson was suffering from a broken collarbone and that he was making it worse by banging his arms against his cage so much.

"He's like a pig in a pen now hisself,"

laughed the Captain. "Well, I guess it's more cooped up like a chicken. Is that irony?"

The cages weren't forever, the Mayor said. She and some of the other grown-ups were thinking of what they called safe, *humane* ways to send the Pig City men downriver. Toward a place called the Gulf of Mexico, they said, or at least Missouri.

The grown-ups had talked a lot in the days after the fight about crossing the river, too. There was no repairing all the smashed windows and smashed-up rooms, the Captain said. But nearer to the Fellowship, there were places. And Arnold Rivers had even let his family eat with the Coalition a few times. Emma told me that Abner had promised to show her the pigs, too, but I don't think Rivers knew about that.

• • •

Beckley came into the Captain's workshop maybe a half-moon after the fight. I'd been weighing a moon's worth of dried food— seeing how much we could take and still get the balloon off the ground. She pointed to the hot air balloon's rainbow-colored top envelope. It was limp, out of air, but patched up.

"So you're definitely going?" Beckley asked.

"The Captain says if I want a lift, it's now or never," I said. "Now that he's able to make it fly, he wants to use the thing. See if he can help more people, maybe go where it's warmer." Beckley didn't reply right away. I took a deep breath. "And . . . it's just that we've seen so much death. I guess I want to go looking for more signs of life."

I set down a sack of dry leeks.

"You're definitely staying?"

Beckley nodded. "I think it'll be good for Emma to be in one place for a while. Even if that place just had to fight off people who wanted to feed us all to pigs. I mean, there are even kids her age here! And with the moving of the camp that's going on . . . I just feel like I can be really useful. It feels like the right time."

"And that boy?" I asked, trying not to smile.

She got red. "And that boy."

From out of her pack, Beckley pulled a battered book. The corners were bent, and white cracks ran across the cover. Her *Gene Matterhorn's Wilderness Survival Guidebook*.

"Here," she said, setting it next to a toolbox. "I think you'll probably need this more than I do. You'll get to be a better reader as you go. And you'd *better* read it. Especially traveling with that lunatic."

"Lunatic?"

"See?" she said. "I'm learning all these cool words, still! No way I could leave Des Moines yet."

After we'd said goodbye and she'd left, the Captain shuffled through the door of his garage, sniffling. He plunked down on his bed and started wiping at his eyes.

"Don't mind me," he said. "It's juss . . . goodbyes, ya know? When Lucas helps us set off tomorrow, I'm gonna be a mess. I've been avoiding that one. Just know I'm gonna get all blubbery."

He plucked a rag from atop his toolbox and blew his nose, smudging black grease across his face.

"You, uh, decided which way we're heading?" I asked.

The Captain grinned and chucked the hat in a corner. "Heh. Warmer climates, Malik, warmer climates. We're gonna see what remains of the fabled southern hospitality. I wonder if anyone still makes bourbon . . ."

"I don't understand most of what you just said."

He unscrewed the top of a safe-to-drink water thermos and poured out a capful, raising it up. "Well, lemme make a toast, then. To broader horizons."

# ABOUT THE AUTHOR

Jonathan Mary-Todd is a writer and vegetarian from Minneapolis.

# The world is over.

## AFTER THE DUST SETTLED

# Can you
# survive
## what's next?

# AFTER THE DUST SETTLED

### Fight the Wind

Fix has a gift for machines. If he can fix up an old wind turbine, he and his friends will be able to live at their Iowa camp for as long as they want. Cleo says no way. She'd rather try to find a city that's rumored to be growing in the southwest. But if another rumor is true—that raiders are heading toward the camp—the only real choice will be fight or die.

### Pig City

Malik and his friends try to avoid cities, but they look for shelter in downtown Des Moines once a winter storm hits. They're quickly trapped in the middle of a struggle between the city's two biggest gangs: the peaceful members of the Coalition and the forces of Pig City, who want to turn everyone else into hog food.

### Plague Riders

When Shep's parents disappeared, he agreed to deliver medicine for the sinister Doctor St. John. The doctor runs the camp of River's Edge with total control, but the pills he makes are the only defense against the nightpox plague. On one trip, Shep learns that his parents may still be alive. With fellow rider Cara by his side, he prepares to escape from River's Edge.